THE OVERMAN

BY

UPTON SINCLAIR

British Library Cataloguing-in-Publication Data
A catalogue record for this book is available from
the British Library

Contents

UPTON SINCLAIR

Upton Sinclair was born in Baltimore, USA in 1878. His alcoholic father moved his family to New York City when Sinclair was ten, where he lived in near-poverty; an experience he later argued contributed to his becoming a socialist. An avid reader, Sinclair was an intelligent child who funded his college education by writing stories for newspapers and magazines. By the age of seventeen, he was earning enough to move into his own apartment. In 1902, he joined the Socialist Party of America, and began to write longer works. However, his first three novels sold badly, despite being favourably received by critics.

Sinclair's first commercial success came in 1906, with the publication of *The Jungle*. A scathing indictment of unregulated capitalism as exemplified by the meat industry – written following seven weeks spent undercover in Chicago's meatpacking plants –

the book was a bestseller. In the months following its publication, domestic and foreign purchases of American meat fell by half, and after reading it, American President Theodore Roosevelt ordered an investigation of the meat-packing industry. Sinclair followed the book with a series of novels which – as with much of his output – were critically well-received, but commercially unsuccessful.

During the twenties, Sinclair continued to produce fiction and engage in socialist political activity, even running as a near-successful candidate for mayor in California. In 1940, his first Lanny Budd novel was published, sparking a series which went on to run for eleven novels. Covering much of the political history of the Western world, all the books were bestsellers, and the third – *Dragon's Teeth* (1942), about the rise of Nazi Germany – won the Pulitzer Prize. Sinclair died in New Jersey in old age.

Upton Sinclair

THE OVERMAN

This is the story of Edward Livingston, as he told it to me only
a few days before he died; he told it as he lay half paralyzed,
and knowing that the hand of death was upon him.

I am by profession a scientist. My story goes back some fifty
years, when I was a student. I had one brother, Daniel Livingston, five years younger than myself, a musician of extraordi-
nary promise. We lived abroad together for a number of years,

each pursuing his own work. About my brother, suffice it to say that music to him was everything – love and friendship, ambition and life. He was a man without a stain, whose lower nature had been burned out by the flame of art. I think the one tie that bound him to the world was myself.

When Daniel Livingston was about twenty-three years of age, his health weakened, and a long sea voyage was decided upon. I could not go with him, so for the first time we parted; and it was twenty years after that before I ever heard of him again.

It was believed that the ship had been wrecked in the South Seas; and I had given him up for dead many years, when it chanced that, as a man advanced in life, I was traveling as a naturalist in Ceylon, and met an old sailor who had been with my brother, and who told me a strange story – how one boat containing five men, including Daniel, had outlived the storm and landed upon an uninhabited island; how, after remaining there for several months, they had made up their minds to risk a voyage in their frail craft; and how my brother alone had refused, declaring his intention to remain by himself, with his violin and the few effects that he had saved.

How this affected me anyone can imagine. The tale was obviously a true one, and I chanced to have means; and so, getting the best idea I could of the island's location, I purchased a yacht outright and prepared to make a search.

The events immediately following bear only indirectly upon my story, and so I pass over them swiftly. We had been at sea for some three weeks, and were in the locality we sought, and watching day and night for some sign of the island, when late one evening the native captain of the vessel came to my cabin, trembling and pale with fright, to tell me that the crew had mutinied and were about to murder me. I rushed to my chest for my revolvers, only to find that every cartridge was gone; and the other's weapon proved to be in the same plight. In this desperate situation the latter suggested what seemed to be the only possible expedient – that we should make our escape from the vessel in the darkness, and trust to gaining the land. While he crept out to provision and lower a boat, I barricaded the cabin-door and waited; and upon hearing the whistle agreed on, I ran to a port-hole, and seeing the boat, slid into it.

An instant later the rope was cut, and I got one glance at the leering countenance of my betrayer, before the ship sped on and all was darkness. I was alone!

The emotions of that night I do not like to recall. Life was still dear to me. It was only when morning came that I lifted my head again and recovered my self-possession.

There was no land in sight – I was tossing upon a waste of water, and already beginning to feel the first cravings of the fearful thirst that I knew must come. But by a strange instinct I still clung to my life; and soon a storm arose, and as the waves began to speed my frail boat along, it rose upon one of them, and I suddenly caught sight of a faint streak of land. I seized the oars and set to work to race for my life. I was not used to the effort, and it took all my strength to keep the craft headed aright, while the sea bore it on to its goal; I fought desperately through the whole day, coming nearer and nearer to my hope, but expecting every instant to be my last, and almost fainting with exhaustion. Finally I came to the very edge of the breakers – and then, in spite of all that I could do, the boat was seized by a wave and whirled round.

I saw before me a long line of bright green forest; and, standing upon the beach in front of me, a single figure – a man – motionless and watching. That moment a breaker smote my little craft, and I was flung into the boiling sea.

I did not know how to swim. I clutched at the boat and missed it, and after that I recall only an instant or two of frantic struggling and choking. When next I opened my eyes, I lay upon the shore, with a man bending over me; and upon my dazed faculties was borne in the startling truth that the man was my brother.

It would have been long before I recognized him but that he was calling me by name. A creature more changed no man could imagine. Gaunt, hollow-eyed, and wild in appearance, he was scarcely the shadow of his former self; he was clad in a rough garment of fur, barefooted and bare-armed, and with long, tangled hair. But what most struck me – what struck me the instant I opened my eyes, and what never ceased to strike me after that – was the strange, haunted look of his whole countenance; his eyes, swift and restless, shone from beneath the shadow of his brows like those of some forest animal.

For the first few dazed minutes I thought of what I had read of men who had gone mad, or had reverted to the beast, under such circumstances as these. Yet nothing could exceed the tenderness of my brother's voice and manner to me; he bent over me with a gourd full of milk, which he helped me to drink, and he dried my face and brushed back the hair from my forehead, whispering to me as one might to a sick child.

I can remember the very words of our conversation at that strange moment, so keenly did every circumstance impress me. I answered him faintly when he asked me how I did, and he pressed my hand. 'You were seeking for me, brother?' he asked.

'I was,' I said.

'I sometimes thought that you might,' he exclaimed. 'Alas! Alas!'

I had been overwhelmed with joy as the truth dawned upon me – the truth that I had found him. I had forgotten our mutual plight. 'Never mind,' I whispered. 'We may get away somehow; and at least we can be together.'

He answered nothing, but helped me lift my head.

'How came you alone in that boat?' he asked.

'It is a long story,' I replied, shuddering as I gazed at the waves that were thundering on the beach before us. 'I will tell it later.'

'You have been long upon the water?'

'Only since last night,' I said; and then gazing about me suddenly, I cried: 'And you – you have been here all these years!'

'All these years,' he answered.

'And alone?'

'Alone.'

I trembled as I gazed into his face; his eyes seemed fairly to burn.

'How have you borne it?' I cried. 'What have you done?'

His answer made me start. 'I have done very well,' he said; 'I have not been unhappy.'

The words seemed strange to me – but his voice was stranger yet. Surely there were signs enough of unhappiness upon his face!

He seemed to read my thoughts. 'Do not worry,' he went on,

pressing his hand in mine; 'I will tell you all about it later.'

But my mind could not be turned away so easily. When I felt stronger and sat up, I came back to the question, gazing at his haggard face and the strange costume he wore.

'You can make no better clothing?' I cried; 'and for food – what do you do?'

'I have all the food that I can eat' was the response, 'and everything else that I need. You shall see.'

'But have you seen *no* one?' I persisted – 'no ships, in all this time?'

'I have not wished to see any,' he said; and then he smiled gently as he saw my stare of amazement. 'I have not wished for anything,' he said gently; 'I have a home, as you shall see, and I have never needed company. Have you forgotten how it used to be, dear brother?'

It took me a long time to understand his words. I was still gazing at him helplessly. 'And you mean,' I cried – 'you mean that you still – you still live in your music?'

'Yes,' he said, 'I mean that.'

I was sitting upright and gripping his arm tightly. 'And for twenty years!' I gasped.

'Twenty thousand years would be all too little for music' was the reply.

I sank back, and he wrapped his arms about me. 'Dear brother,' he said, smiling, 'let us not go into that just now. Wait until tomorrow, at the least. Perhaps I can help you now, and we can walk.'

We had not far to go, and with his help I managed the task. Back from the shore rose a high cliff, and a cavern in this was evidently his home. At one side there was a pen, in which were three or four captive goats; and upon the grassy lawn in front was a rough seat. With the exception of a fireplace, and a path he had cut through the thicket, there were no other signs that the place was inhabited.

I sank down upon the grass, and he brought me fresh water and fruits, and cooked rice, which I ate hungrily. Then, when I was stronger, I got up and began to examine his home.

The cave was the size of a large room; it was dry, but bare of all furniture except a table and a roughly made chair and bed. My brother's possessions consisted mainly of a few objects (notably some tools) which he and the sailors had been able to recover from the wreck of the ship. There were a few skins which served him as bags in which to keep his provisions; his bowls and dishes were gourds and the shells of turtles. He was without artificial light, and he had only a few quires of writing-paper from the ship-captain's portfolio. For the rest, a violin without strings, and a bow without hairs, made up a list of the possessions so far as I could make them out. And it was upon the strength of these that he had said to me: 'I have everything that I need'!

With rest and food my strength returned, and before long my mind was altogether occupied with my brother.

First of all, of course, my thought was of his home – of his surroundings and his ways. I rummaged about his cavern, wondering at his makeshifts – or, rather, at his lack of them.

'You have no lamp?' I cried. 'But, Daniel, the wax-plant grows in this climate. Or you might use tallow or oil.'

'Dear brother,' he answered, 'you forget that I have no books to read. And the few things that need light – cannot I just as well do them by day?'

'But then, the long nights – you sleep?'

'No,' said he gently, 'I do not sleep'; and then, with his strange smile, he added: 'I live.'

'You live!' I echoed in perplexity; and then I stopped, catching the quiet, steady gaze of his eyes.

'Just so,' he said, 'I live. I had never lived before.'

Most of all, I think, I was perplexed at the sight of his violin. From what I had seen of his youthful life, I could have imagined him spending all day and all night with that; but here it hung, useless as a stick of wood.

'You could have made strings for it,' I said. 'I can make them for you.'

'But they would be of no use to me,' he answered.

'And all your music – you have given it up?'

'The music I have to do with,' he said, 'has long ceased to be music that anyone could play.'

'But Daniel!' I protested.

'Listen to me,' he said. 'Have you never read that Beethoven never heard some of his greatest symphonies? Do you not understand how a musician can comprehend music from a score? And from that, how he can create it in his own mind and enjoy it, without ever writing it down or hearing it?'

'Then,' I said, almost speechless with wonder; 'then you compose music in your mind?'

'No,' he said. 'I *live* music in my soul.'

These things were on the day after my rescue, after I had recovered from my exhaustion. The words which he spoke I no more comprehended than if I had been a child; but the strangeness of the thing haunted my soul, and my questioning and arguing never ceased. All of this he bore with a gentle patience.

I had my youthful recollections of Robinson Crusoe; and as a man of science, I could naturally not spend two minutes conversing with Daniel and examining his affairs without thinking of some new device by which he could have made his lot more tolerable. I could as yet hardly realize that it was to be my own fate to live upon the deserted island forever; all my thoughts were of what I should have done had I been in his place. He had no weapons, no traps, no gardens, no house – and so on. 'But Edward,' he would say again and again, 'do you not understand? Once more – I have no *time* for such things.'

'Time! *Time!*' I would cry. 'But what *else* have you? What have you to *do?*'

'I have my life to live' was the invariable response; 'I have no time for anything else.'

We were sitting that afternoon beneath the shade of a great forest-tree before the cavern. Suddenly, seeing again the dazed look upon my face, he put his arm about me.

'Listen to me, dear brother,' he said, smiling. 'You remember Diogenes, who lived in a tub? That was in order that he might have to call no man master, and no thing – least of all his own body. And can you not see that a man's own soul is his soul just the same, whether he be on a desert island or in the midst of a city of millions? And that mind, emotion, will – he has the life of his soul to live?'

I sat surprised into silence; then suddenly I felt Daniel's arm tighten about me. 'Ah, my dear brother,' he said, his voice lowering, 'it will be so hard! Do you think I have not realized it – how hard, *hard* it will be?'

'What will be hard?' I asked.

'Your life – everything you have to face,' he answered. 'How can you not see it – do you not see that *you* have to live upon this island, too?'

'I have not thought of it much,' I said. 'I have been thinking of you.'

'I know it,' he replied; 'but I do not see how you are to bear it. I saw it all while I watched you sweep in with the boat – I saw all the pain and all the sorrow, and it was long before I made up my mind that it was not best to let you die.'

I started, but he held me tight.

'Yes,' he said, 'and I fear that I chose wrongly. Is it not strange that a man who has seen what I have seen should still be bound by such chains – that what I knew would be best, I could not do, simply because you were my brother?'

He must have felt my heart beating faster. 'Listen to me,' he went on quickly, but still with his frightful quietness. 'Listen to me while I try to tell you – what I can hardly bear to tell you. All the tragedy of being is summed up in such a situation as this of ours; I am as helpless before it as you are – both of us are as helpless as children.'

I gazed at him again, and suddenly he caught me with the wild look of his eyes. He had no need to hold me with his hand.

'Brother,' he said, 'you must think this out for yourself, as you can: I cannot explain it to you – cannot explain anything about it. Suffice it to say that for twenty years I have lived here, and that I have fought a fight which no man has ever fought before, and seen what I believe no man has ever seen. Knowing you as I do, I know that you can by no possibility ever follow me. It is as if I had found the fourth dimension of space; it is as if I dwelt in a house through the walls of which you walked without seeing them. How you are to bear your life here, my dear, dear brother, I do not know; but the truth is merciless, and you must face it – you will have to live on this island all your days, I am sure; and you will have to live here *alone!*'

A sudden shudder passed through me. 'Daniel!' I gasped; it seemed to me that his eyes were on fire. 'You mean, I suppose, that you are going away to some other part of the place – to another island?'

'Whether I go to another place or not, what matters that?

No, I shall not, I think; and rest assured that, whatever I do, I love you, my heart yearns for you, and all my tenderness and love are yours; but also that though you were with me, and held me in your arms four-and-twenty hours a day – yet all the time you would be alone.'

I could find no word to say – I could scarcely think.

'The pain of it,' he went on, still quietly, still tenderly, 'is that I cannot explain it to anyone, that I cannot explain it to myself; that there are no words for it, nothing but the thing. The only explanation I can give is that I am become a madman, and that you must accept the fact. For the thing I do I can no more help doing than I could help the beating of my heart. All the world of love that I might bear to you, or to any other human soul, could no more enable me to stop than it would enable the grass to stop growing. Again you must accept the fact – you must learn to think of me as a man who is in the grasp of a fiend.'

There was a pause. Not once had I taken my eyes from my brother's, and I sat with my heart throbbing wildly; the strangeness of the whole thing was too much for me – at times I was certain that I was indeed listening to a maniac.

When my brother began speaking again, I was at first hardly conscious of it. 'Edward,' he said, 'I have thought about this – that perhaps my presence would be painful to you. If so, let me go away. Take what tools I have here, and make this place your home – you have knowledge at your command, you can plant and hunt and study, and do what you will. As for me, such things make no difference; I could soon make myself comfortable again, and perhaps—'

'Say no more about it,' I interrupted quickly; 'if anyone must go, let it be me, for I shall have need of occupation.'

For long hours after that strange experience I was pacing up and down the storm-swept beach of the island. What I had heard had disturbed me more than anything before in my life; the whole surroundings contributed to the effect – the perils I had passed through, the terrible future which stretched before me, the loss of my brother, and the finding of this strange madman in his place. But I was by nature a practical person, scientific and precise in my mode of thought; I did my best to convince myself that solitude and suffering had unhinged my brother's mind. There is no use telling a scientist that he cannot understand a certain matter, and expecting him to let it rest; my mind was soon made up that I would study this malady, and perhaps cure it. My interest in the strange problem did more than anything else to keep me from realizing to the full extent the discomfort I must needs face in the future.

When hunger brought my thoughts back to myself, I returned to the cave, where I found my brother pacing backward and forward upon a path which he had worn deep in the ground in front of his home; his head was sunk forward, his eyes on the ground, and he was evidently lost in deep thought. I spoke to him once, but he did not hear me; I walked by him and entered the cavern.

I now set to work to make a thorough examination of his belongings, musing that perhaps the best way to get to the bottom of his strange trouble would be to provide him with some of the ordinary amenities of life. I found that the tools were not too rusty to be of service, and being a person with a talent for doing things, I was soon interested in planning how I could make a habitable place out of the cave. In the latitude I knew that a door and a fireplace would never be an absolute necessity; but I pleased myself thinking that they might not be useless when the storms blew in. Also, being blessed with much knowledge of the natural world, I flattered myself that before many days would have passed I should have added considerably to the comforts of the house.

I gave the balance of the day to a preliminary ransacking of the island. A scientist has an inexhaustible mine of interest in such an environment, and in the plans which I formed for work I forgot everything else for the time.

And so towards sundown I returned to the cabin. My brother was still pacing to and fro, exactly as I had left him. Taught by previous experience, I entered the cabin without addressing him, and set about preparing a meal. I had not gone very far before I heard his step behind me.

'Edward,' he said.

'What is it?' I asked, turning.

'I wished merely to tell you – that you will not see me for a day or two. I wish you not to worry about me.'

I gazed at him in perplexity that was too great to permit of my framing a question. His haggard glance met mine again, and again he put his hand upon my shoulder with a gesture of affection; then he turned and went slowly away.

The incident diminished my appetite, for I had expected to interest him in my banquet. I sat for hours afterwards, gazing out of the cavern entrance at the moon-lighted grove, silent and desolate beyond any telling. I think I never felt more alone than just then.

The problem was my only company; I had no idea where Daniel had gone; but after a feverish sleep I was up again at dawn, my mind fully made up for a search. I fear I drag out my story – it was nearly sundown when at last my efforts were rewarded. I was returning home in despair and misery, when, suddenly, in the back of the same cliffs in which was our home, I saw another opening, and with a gleam of hope I hurried towards it and peered in. It was too dark to see, but I entered and stepped to one side in the darkness; and then, as my eyes adjusted themselves to the gloom, I saw my brother.

I was unperceived, and I went forward until I could see him plainly. He sat upon a block of stone, the edge of which his hands gripped tensely; with his face slightly raised, he was staring before him into space. I would describe, if I could, the impression which his whole appearance gave me; it was of a man undergoing some fearful strain. The knotted muscles stood out upon his arms; his nostrils were distended, his breath coming fast, and I could see the veins throbbing in his forehead. I stood for I know not how long, with my heart beating madly, a strange, indescribable *fear* in possession of me. Divining the truth instinctively, I moved in front of him and gazed into his eyes; he neither saw me nor heard me, nor gave any sign that he was conscious of my presence. Then suddenly, unable to bear the strain any longer, I clutched him in my arms, crying wildly: 'Daniel! Daniel!'

To my horror, he gave no signs. Even then I clung to him, I shook him; I could feel the quivering of his tense arms. At last, completely overcome, I turned and staggered from the place.

All that night I lay stretched out upon the bed, sleepless. I had studied medicine, but nothing that I had ever heard of bore any resemblance to this. Perhaps two hours after sunrise, as I was sitting with my eyes fixed in the direction of the other cavern, all at once I saw my brother appear.

I sprang up in sheer fright; he was pale beyond imagination. He paid no attention to me, but went past me and entered the cave. He groped his way to his larder and, sinking down upon the ground, took some of the food and ate it slowly. There was a bowl of milk which I had put there, and which he drank. Then he lay down, resting his head upon his arm, and fell fast asleep.

I followed him in silence when he rose, his weakness apparently gone. He went to the spring which was near the cavern, and bathed his face and arms in the stream below it. After that he came towards me and, sitting down beside me, put his arm around me.

'Dear brother,' he said, 'it was very good of you; but please do not do what you did again.'

'You knew that I was there?' I cried.

'Yes,' he said, 'I knew it.'

'And why did you not answer me?'

'I could not answer you, brother.' And then with a sudden gesture he checked me. 'I could not even tell you *why*,' he said. 'It must suffice you, Edward, to know that this must be, and that you cannot help it.'

'But it will kill me!' I cried.

'Perhaps,' he said very quietly, 'or perhaps it will kill me first. I cannot tell.'

We stood for some minutes without speaking. 'Daniel,' I ventured at last, 'I had hoped that in the external ways I might assist you – your food, perhaps—'

'I could not let you serve me,' he answered; 'I have no way to serve you in return. And, besides that, I have learned to do cheerfully what little physical toil I must. The island is covered with food, you know.'

'But if you should be sick?' I cried.

'If I should be sick,' he said, 'I should either get well again, or else die.'

'Then you do not feel pain?'

'To learn to bear pain has been one of my tasks' was the response. 'I should think,' he continued, changing the subject abruptly, 'that if you had studied all your life as you did when we lived together, by this time you would not fear solitude – that you would find in this new world enough to fill all your time.'

'I might – perhaps I shall,' I said; 'but Daniel, you have been here twenty years, and never seen a ship! So how could I know that the result of any studies of mine would ever be made known to the world? I have not even any paper to write upon.'

The other sat gazing ahead of him at the moonlit water through the trees; I saw the strange smile upon his lips again.

'All that sorrow,' he said. 'I fought with it once myself, and how I wish that I could help you to fight with it! For a year or so I also waited for a ship, and wrote down the best of my music, and poured out the tears of my soul. But, Edward, I no longer write my music, and I no longer fear lest my work be not made known to the world.'

His voice had sunk low. Over the tree-tops a silver moon was gleaming, and his eyes were fixed upon it. 'On that huge ball of iron and rock,' said he, 'there was once power and life and beauty; and now it rolls there through the years and the ages, cold and dead and still. And some day this planet, too, will roll through the years and the ages; and no eye will behold it, and no mind will be aware of it; and the voices of men will be hushed upon it, and the monuments of men will be dust upon it; and, Edward, what then of my music, what then of your science and your books?'

I answered nothing.

'Perhaps in all the ages that have gone over this island,' he continued, 'no human foot ever trod upon it before.'

And so my brother passed on, pressing his hand upon my shoulder; and through the watches of the night I saw him pacing backward and forward, backward and forward, upon the long, white stretch of sand.

A month must have passed after that – I took little heed of the time. I toiled at the cave, I played hunter and naturalist. I was busy with my hands, but very seldom was I happy or at peace. For day after day that silent figure roamed here and there before my eyes, and hour after hour those strange, silent vigils to the black cavern continued. I grew more and more restless and oppressed, until at last, one night, at the end of a long and exhausting vigil, my impatience reached its climax.

I remember how I sat by his side and caught his hand, like a supplicating child. 'Daniel,' I asked, 'has it never occurred to you that you are unkind to me?'

'Unkind?' he asked gently.

'Unkind,' I said. 'I have waited – how long have I waited! It seemed to me that it could not last forever – that you would not continue to treat me always as if I were a child.'

'Edward,' he said, 'I know what you are going to say. I wish that you would spare me.'

'I cannot spare you!' I cried with sudden vehemence. 'I tell you I cannot bear it – I tell you I shall go mad! This loneliness and this haunting perplexity – I swear to you that I cannot endure it any longer!'

My brother sat gazing before him. After a moment I went on, more quietly, pleading with him. 'Daniel,' I said, 'you cannot ever persuade me that you must needs treat me as you have treated me since I came to this place. I came here to seek for you – for that purpose alone – and with love in my heart. And you keep me from you, you treat me as if I were not a human being!'

'Stop, Edward!' cried my brother imploringly. 'Do not say such things as that! Ah! what can I tell you? How can I say it to you? It is not enough that you should be a human being.'

'Not enough!' I echoed.

'Ah! do you suppose – can you suppose – that if this thing of which we speak were mine to give – if by losing it myself I could give it to you – can you suppose I would not do it, and do it with joy? All that love could make possible I would do – how much I would do I cannot tell you. But this that you ask of me – this I *cannot* do!'

'You mean' – I clung to the argument with my scientific instinct – 'you mean that there is in your own life, in your own mind, certain things which could be conveyed to another's?'

'I do,' he said.

'But the use of words—' I began.

'No words could have any relation to this,' he said.

'But ideas, Daniel!' I protested. 'There may be ideas in the mind for which we can find no words, but surely we can approximate them, we can foreshadow them.'

'There are some things in my mind that are not ideas' was his quick reply.

'I do not understand that,' I exclaimed.

'I know it,' said my brother; 'that is the point.'

'But,' I cried in vexation, 'but what could such things be? How can one think—'

' "In that high hour thought was not," ' my brother quoted.

I sat silent, and a long pause followed. Then I began once more: 'Let me ask you, Daniel; perhaps you do not understand how difficult it is for one mind to believe that it cannot grasp what is in another mind. But this – this knowledge to which you have come – you must surely have come to it by degrees, by a process?'

'Yes,' said he.

'And of that – surely you could explain to me at least the beginning, which might help me to divine in what the difference consists?'

He answered nothing for a moment. I went on quickly: 'Ah, I fear that there must be another reason that you do not realize. Might it not be true that you would find it easier to explain to another than to me? Is it not at all that you shrink from my ways of thinking? Is it not that you know that I have never understood your art?'

'Tell me,' he asked suddenly, 'what have you thought about me since you have been here?'

'What difference does it make what I think?' I cried. 'What data have I for thinking anything? I know that I am in the presence of something which haunts me; and also that I have never been more wretched in my life.

'Ah, Daniel!' I cried, 'be fair with me – you have not been fair! Why should you shrink from me as if I were a base person? What harm could it do, even if I did not understand you? I cannot help it – the effect of this thing upon me; I am a grown man, and yet you have turned me into a child again! If you were to tell me about ghosts, I think I should take it for the truth.'

'Ah!' said my brother.

'Yes, even that!' I cried. 'But you think I am not worthy even to guess at your life and your knowledge – no, do not try to stop me, I know that this is the fact! If it were not so, you would trust to love – you would not cast me away from you, you would do what you could!'

'Be still! Be still!' he whispered. 'Do not speak to me that way – I will do what I can – I will tell you what I am able.'

For a long time he sat with knit brows. Then at last he began his story.

'I go back,' he said, 'to the time when I first landed on this island. The ship was wrecked upon the bar just ahead of us; and later, when the sea fell, we set to work to save from it as much as we could. The voyage had restored my health, and I had my violin; and when I ascertained that the place sheltered no wild beasts or men, I was myself well content to remain as long as might be necessary. I had no doubt that some ship would appear in the end; and meanwhile there was nothing to trouble me, except the enforced companionship of men who did not understand me. In the end, I escaped from that trouble with the plea that if I took up my residence at the other side of the island, I could better watch the sea; and so I built a tiny hut, and was, I think, as happy as I had ever been before.

'But as the months passed by and no vessel appeared, the situation changed. I perceived that sooner or later my violin would be useless; and about the same time the sailors came to me to say that they had decided to rig a boat with a sail, and endeavor to reach some inhabited island. It was the time of quiet seas, and they preferred to run the risk to remaining longer in isolation.

'I was then called upon to make the great decision. Should I chance my life with the rest, or should I trust to the certainty that some day a vessel would appear, and meanwhile devote myself to the work which loomed before me – the living of my life, the seeking of the power which I felt to be hidden in me, without any external assistance or reference whatever? Perhaps, had I seen the twenty years before me, I should have shrunk from the task; but, as it was, I chose what was to be the bolder, to my companions the more timid course.

'After that, of course, there could be no halfway measures. I had to make good my purpose; I had to face either absolute victory or absolute defeat. As I had expected, my violin soon became useless, and, no ship appearing, I perceived in the end that I had to give up that thought, too.

'I have already hinted the grounds of my argument to you. It is my belief that life is its own end, and needs no justification. It is also my belief that each individual soul is a microcosm, self-sufficient, and its own excuse for being. Each day as I wrought, I came to be more and more possessed with that truth; it came to be more and more self-evident and final; until at last there came a day when I would not have hailed a ship had I seen one – when the life that loomed up before me within my own heart was a thing of so much interest that the rest of the world was nothing in comparison.

'At first I had felt just as you feel now – I had been interested in food and clothing and light, and what not else; but in the end I found myself behaving as a soldier upon a long campaign – I strewed my path with the things that had once been necessities, and that now were encumbrances. It proved thus with my violin – strings or no strings; the music that throbbed in my soul and swept me away into the far spaces of my being – it was no longer to be limited and restrained by what human fingers could achieve. It was as if I had once plodded upon the land and now discovered wings. When the vision came to me, I no longer toiled for weeks to shape it and record it – I went on where the new light shone, where the new hope beckoned; and so, day after day, toward things with which it is not easy for words to deal.'

My brother paused for a while; I did not speak.

'When I try to talk with you of these things,' he said at last, 'I do not know where I stand. I find myself thinking of the brother I remember – who was content to call himself a materialist. You ask me what was this life that I speak of – was it thought, was it emotion, was it will? It was all, I think; always it involved contemplation, the beholding of a universe of being, and the comprehending of it as an utterance of power; and always it was emotion, the flooding of one's being with an oceantide of joy and exultation; and always it was will – it was the concentration of all the powers of one's soul in one colossal effort. But chiefest of all, I think – and what is hardest even to hint at – it was the fourth, and the highest of the faculties of the mind – it was imagination.

'It is endless – that is the first thing that a man learns about it – it is the very presence of the infinite. And also he learns that it is at his command – that it is no accident, but his being itself; that he has but to call, and it comes; that he has but to knock, and it is opened unto him. It is that for which pilgrims and crusaders have fought, which prophets and saints have sung.

And it is that, of course, which is the life of music. Music lies nearest to this mystery; to him who understands, it is the living presence of the spirit. Its movement is the building up of that ecstasy, its complexity is the infiniteness of that vision – all the fullness and the wonder and the glory of it are there.'

I give but my recollection of my brother's words. He paused again and sat gazing before him. 'I do not know,' he said, 'how much these metaphors convey to you. A long time had passed – some eight years, I imagine, though I kept no count of the time. I was coming bit by bit to a new and strange experience – which is not of this life, and one which would seem to you, I imagine, as altogether supernatural.

'So,' said Daniel, 'you must believe me as you can. I have spoken of strange bursts of vision, sudden gleams of insight which shake one's being to its depth. Such experiences are not unusual – poets have sung of them; but now there came to be something which, strange as it may sound, seemed to be not of a kind with my own soul – something which affected me with an indescribable *fear*. I fought against the thought, for I had no belief in the unseen. I strive to put into words something that cannot be put into words – but I was like a man groping in utter darkness, and touching something *alive*. I had fought my way into this unknown land, and everywhere I had gone, so far, the things that I achieved were of my own power, the impulses were those of my own will. But now, day by day, I was haunted by the unthinkable suspicion that into my life was coming something that was not myself. I was a bird mounting upon the air – and the air had a will of its own! It was something that repelled me – something that drew me. I wrestled with the thought day and night, comparing it with anything of which I had ever heard or known. But in vain – it was new to me.

'These things of which I speak you must understand as happening in the midst of a tempest of emotions; I sat in a state which there is no imagining – I ate nothing for days, I sat for days without moving, until at last there came the climax, a desperate resolve, a mounting up, a battling with unseen forces, a knocking upon unseen doors – and then a sudden rending away of barriers, and the inpourings of a sea of life. I can only use metaphors. I was a traveler, and I had toiled towards the sunrise, climbing peak upon peak, and suddenly I had stepped out upon the summit, and stood transfixed with the glory of an endless vision of dawn.'

My brother's voice had sunk to a whisper, and his hand lay upon my arm. I cannot tell how his words had affected me.

'And this – this thing—' I ventured. 'It is real?'

'It is real,' he said. 'There is nothing else so real.'

'And it – it is a heaven?'

'No,' he said, 'it is another earth.'

I started.

'As a scientist,' he said, 'what do you believe about the universe? Is there life throughout it?'

'I do not know. It is a possibility.'

'Yes,' said Daniel, 'but for me it is a certainty. It is a fact in which I live, day after day.'

I had caught him by the arm.

'Daniel!' I cried.

'It is just so,' he said.

'Another planet?'

'I do not know' was the answer. 'Another race of beings, is all that I can tell you.'

'And are they human beings?'

'They have passed entirely beyond anything which those words can mean to me.'

'And you know them?'

'Yes.'

'And personally?'

'More than personally.'

'How do you mean?'

'I know them directly. I live in their lives. I know them as I know the symphony I hear – as one drop of water knows the sea.'

I was dazed; I could hardly think. 'And their name?' I asked.

'They have no name,' said my brother, 'they have no words. They have passed the need of language – they communicate with each other by immediate spiritual union. Their life is upon a higher plane than ours; they do not deal in ideas, but in imaginative intuitions.'

'And then, Daniel, when you – when you pass into that trance – it is that!'

'It is that,' said he. 'By an effort of my will I lift myself into their consciousness; but because my physical and mental faculties have not been prepared by long ages of development, my time with them is limited, and I fall back to recruit my strength.'

'And this has been going on for years?'

'For ten or twelve years' was his reply.

It will, perhaps, be best for me to give the substance of what he told me in the long conversation which ensued. 'I do not know where these people are,' he told me. 'I only know that throughout universal space they are the race which is nearest in its development to our own. I do not know what they look like. I have never seen nor heard them. I only live their lives. I do not ask them any questions; our relation is nothing of that sort. It is as if they were playing music which I heard; but also as if their music was their whole life, so that I know all they have and do. Their presence comes to me as the inwelling of universal joy; of love and worship and rapture, unending and unthinkable. Their life is infinite variety – immediate and perpetual expansion – spiritual insight developing in a ratio determined by the will of the individuals. It is as if a man were to witness the springtime arising of Nature, but taking place in an hour instead of three months; and he comprehending it, not from the outside, but living it, as a bursting forth of song.'

'And to this song there is no limit?' I asked him.

'When you speak of the soul as being infinite,' said Daniel, 'you do not mean that it extends merely beyond your thoughts, but you mean that you may heap quantity upon quantity, and multiply quantity by quantity, in any ratio and at any speed you please, and still have infinity before you.'

'You mean that these beings understand what is going on in each other's mind?'

'They understand all minds as you understand your own. It is of the nature of spiritual passion to mingle at a certain stage of intensity, like electricity in the lightning flash. This race has developed a new sense, just as man has developed senses which are not possessed by lower animals.'

'And these people were once men?'

'Presumably.'

'And then they have escaped altogether from the sorrows of life?'

'Say, rather,' he answered, 'that they have escaped to the sorrows of life. The essence of life is sorrow.'

'It does not seem so, from your picture,' I said.

'That is simple, because my picture is not understood. Every one of these beings of whom I speak bears in his bosom a pain for which there are no words; every one of them – there are countless numbers of them, living each in my consciousness as the voice of one instrument lives in a symphony – each one is a Titan spirit, wrestling day and night without end, without possibility of respite, and bearing on his shoulders a universal load of woe. In no way could you imagine one better than as a soldier in the crisis of the battle, panting, and blind with pain, dying amid the glory of his achievement.'

'And such a life!' I cried. 'Why do they live it?'

'They live it because it demands with the voice of all their being to be lived; because the presence of it is rapture and unutterable holiness; because it will allow no questions, because it is instant, imperative, and final – *it will be lived!*'

I sat in silence. 'Do I gather from your words,' I asked, 'that immortality is not one of the privileges of this race?'

He smiled again. 'The spiritual life,' he said, 'does not begin until the thought of immortality is flung away. A man's duty looms up before him – and in his weakness he will not do it, but puts the fruition of his life into another world, where the terms are not so hard!'

'This people,' I asked, 'what do they know about God?'

'They know no more than men do' was the answer, 'except that they know they know nothing. They know that the veil is not lifted. It is not that for which they seek – life is their task, and life only; to behold its endless fruition; to dwell in the beauty of it, to wield power of it; to toil at its whirling loom, to build up palaces of music from it. Ah, my brother, why have you never lived a symphony?'

'These people have no physical life?' I asked.

'Assuredly they have' was his answer, 'but it is a life which does not enter their consciousness – any more than, for instance, the beating of your heart and the renewing of your tissues. They have attained to mastery over the world of matter. They temper the seasons to their wish; disease and ill-health they have banished entirely; and, understanding the ways of Nature, they create their food at will.'

'And their society knows no rich and no poor? Their government?'

'They have no government,' he said; 'their law is their inspiration.'

Until far into the night we sat talking; and then, early in the morning, as I went out upon the beach – I saw a ship standing in towards the shore! I recall, as if it were yesterday, how my heart leaped up, and with what an agony of uncertainty I stood waving a signal.

And then I rushed to see my brother, shouting the news aloud. Startled with his own thoughts, he gazed at me in perplexity.

'A ship has come!' I cried. 'A ship!'

'A ship!' he echoed; and then, with a sudden light: 'Oh, I see!'

'Come!' I cried. 'They will take us aboard!'

But my brother shook his head. 'No, Edward,' he replied, 'I cannot do that.'

I started. 'No,' he said again, 'do not ask me. You go – but let me stay here until the end!'

'What can you mean?' I cried. 'Can you really suppose that I would leave you?'

'I am not fitted to travel,' he said. 'I do not wish to change. And I could not face the thing which you call civilization. It has no interest for me.'

'But we can live in the country,' I cried. 'I have money – nothing need trouble you!' But all my arguments made no impression upon him; he would only repeat that he desired to be left alone. I tried to move him by saying that I would not leave him. I might stay if I chose, he said – he could not help that – but if I were wise, I would leave him to his own life; and I would not subject him to the pain of meeting the strangers upon the ship. They would not understand, and they would only cause him vexation. And even while I was protesting with him, we heard the shouts of men upon the shore. He rose up and laid his hand upon my shoulder, and kissed me upon the forehead, saying: 'Be wise – or let me be wise for you. Respect my judgment and let me go.'

And so he turned and started away towards the centre of the island. At the edge of the thicket he turned and waved his hand to me. I never saw him again.